P9-CJK-783

PUBLISHED BY SLEEPING BEAR PRESS

It has pages and pictures,
a cover, it's true,
even words and a writer—
and readers like you.

It can do anything
that you want it to do.
It's more than just a book.

Because books do not have wings.

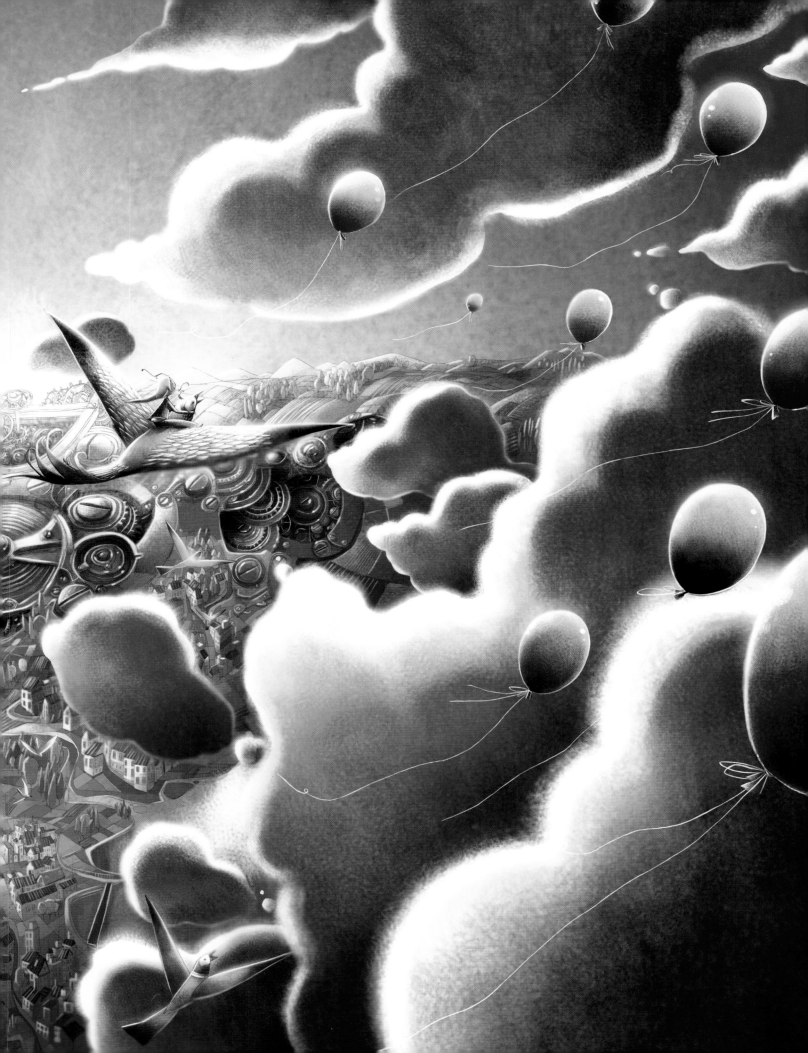

Books don't have engines
or trampoline springs.
And this, for certain,
has all of those things.

This is a sculpture,
some fine work of art,
a puzzle assembled
for taking apart.
It plumps up your thinker
and fills up your heart.
And where you end up
is not where you start.

Surely, it's more than a book.

It can be a port of sorts,
the dip of a ship on a trip, of course,
a passage by pirates
to faraway forts.

This, here, is a submarine,
a never-look-back, pretend-it machine,
to explore the depths
of the vast marine
with urchins, seaweed,
and schools of sardines.

Come closer, dear reader,
and see the unseen—
this thing that's not just a book.

If you look, you will see
it's a cunning old shrew
with a bubbling brew
of lizard stew,
tapping the toe
of her crooked shoe,
planning potions for ogres
and princesses, too.

Suppose it's the gleam
of a dream, instead,
nestled inside a dragon's head
who sleeps in the sky
with clouds for a bed
and stuffs stars with wishes
that fly overhead.

Though it comes to an end,
do not be misled.
This is not just a book.

It's a flock of fairies
chatting with trees
and painting the colors
on lilies and leaves,
dusting the forest,
enchanted with glee,
singing together
in twos and in threes.

It's older than old
and newer than new.
It can't be what it is
without someone like you.

I'll tell you again—
it's the truest of true.
It's certainly more than a book.

If it's not what it's not,
then what could it be—
spectacles, perhaps,
that might help you see?

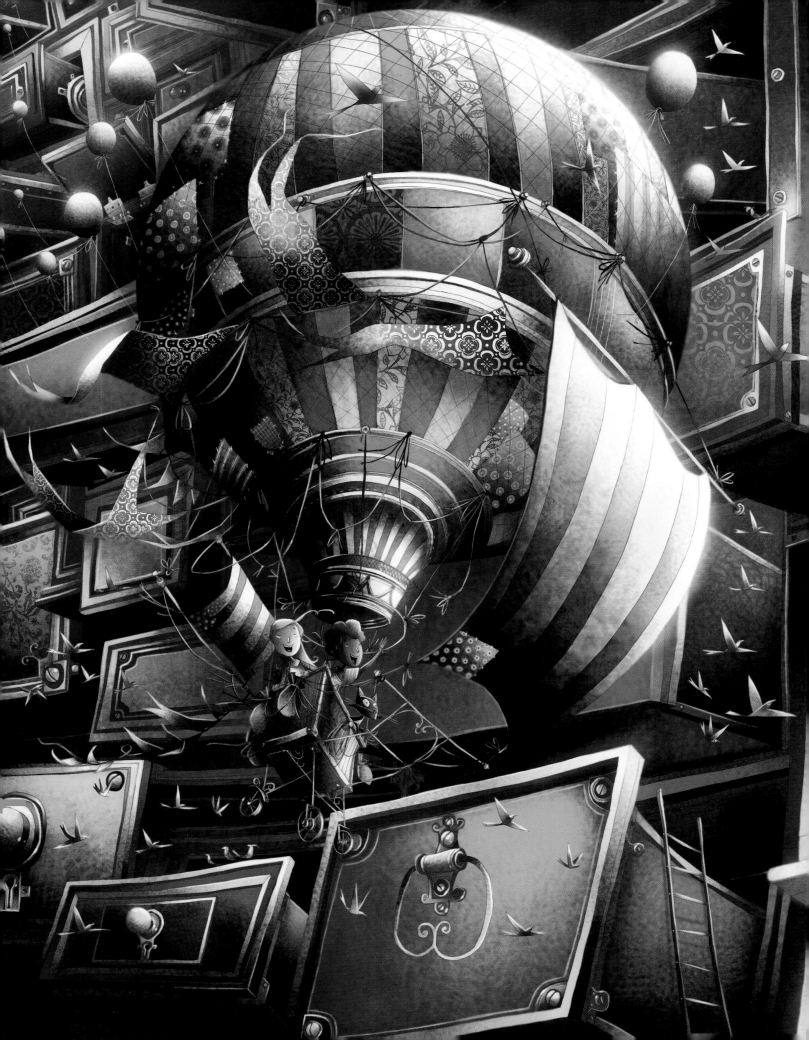

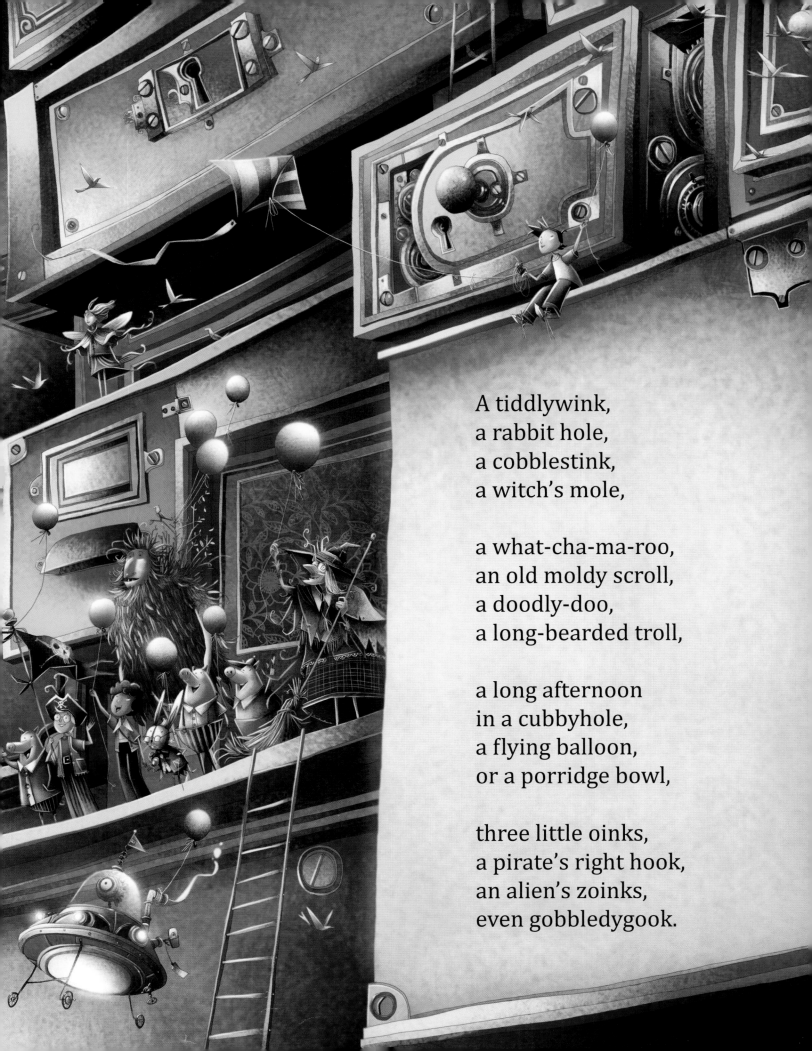

A tiddlywink,
a rabbit hole,
a cobblestink,
a witch's mole,

a what-cha-ma-roo,
an old moldy scroll,
a doodly-doo,
a long-bearded troll,

a long afternoon
in a cubbyhole,
a flying balloon,
or a porridge bowl,

three little oinks,
a pirate's right hook,
an alien's zoinks,
even gobbledygook.

A book is a book
when all by itself,
when it's closed and flat,
alone on the shelf.

If, and only if,
you don't care to look,
then, and only then,
will it *just* be . . .
a book.